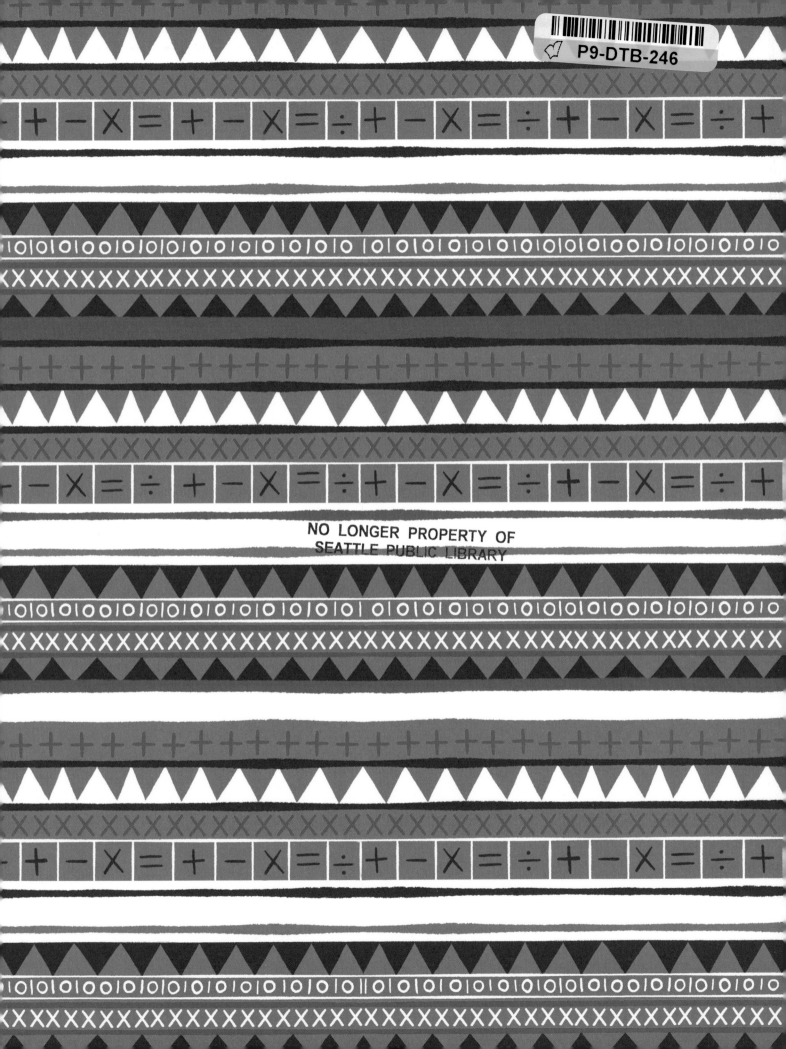

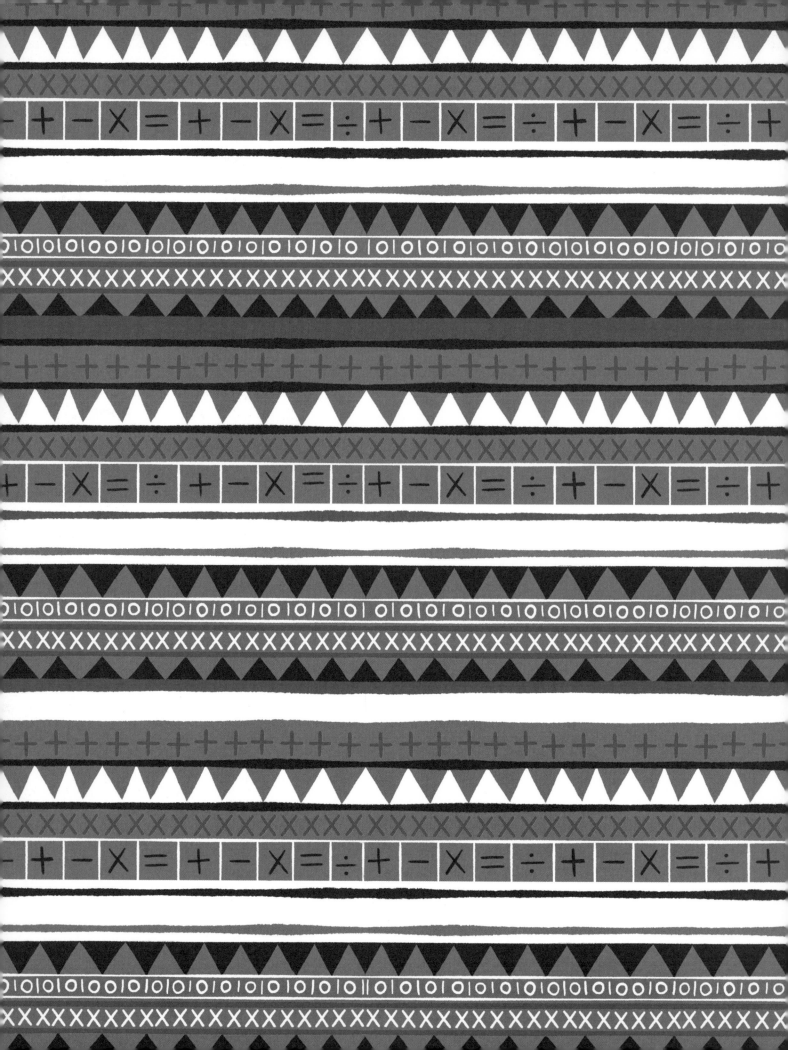

Bears Make the Best MATH BUDDIES

written by
CARMEN OLIVER

illustrated by
JEAN CLAUDE

CAPSTONE EDITIONS
a capstone imprint

Bears Make the Best Math Buddies is published by
Capstone Editions, a Capstone imprint
1710 Roe Crest Drive
North Mankato, Minnesota 56003
www.mycapstone.com

Library of Congress Cataloging-in-Publication Data
is available on the Library of Congress website.

ISBN 978-1-68446-079-3 (hardcover)

Summary: Adelaide and Bear have tackled reading together,
and now they are tackling math. Adelaide stands up
for her best friend and his many talents, but will she
convince her teacher to let Bear be her math buddy?

Printed and bound in China.
1667

"It's time for our math lesson. Everyone pair up with a buddy," said Mrs. Fitz-Pea.

Everyone did—except Adelaide.

"Oh dear," said Mrs. Fitz-Pea. "We have a problem. We're short one student."

"Don't worry," said Adelaide. "I have the answer."

$1 +$

$2 + $

$3 + $

$4 + 3$

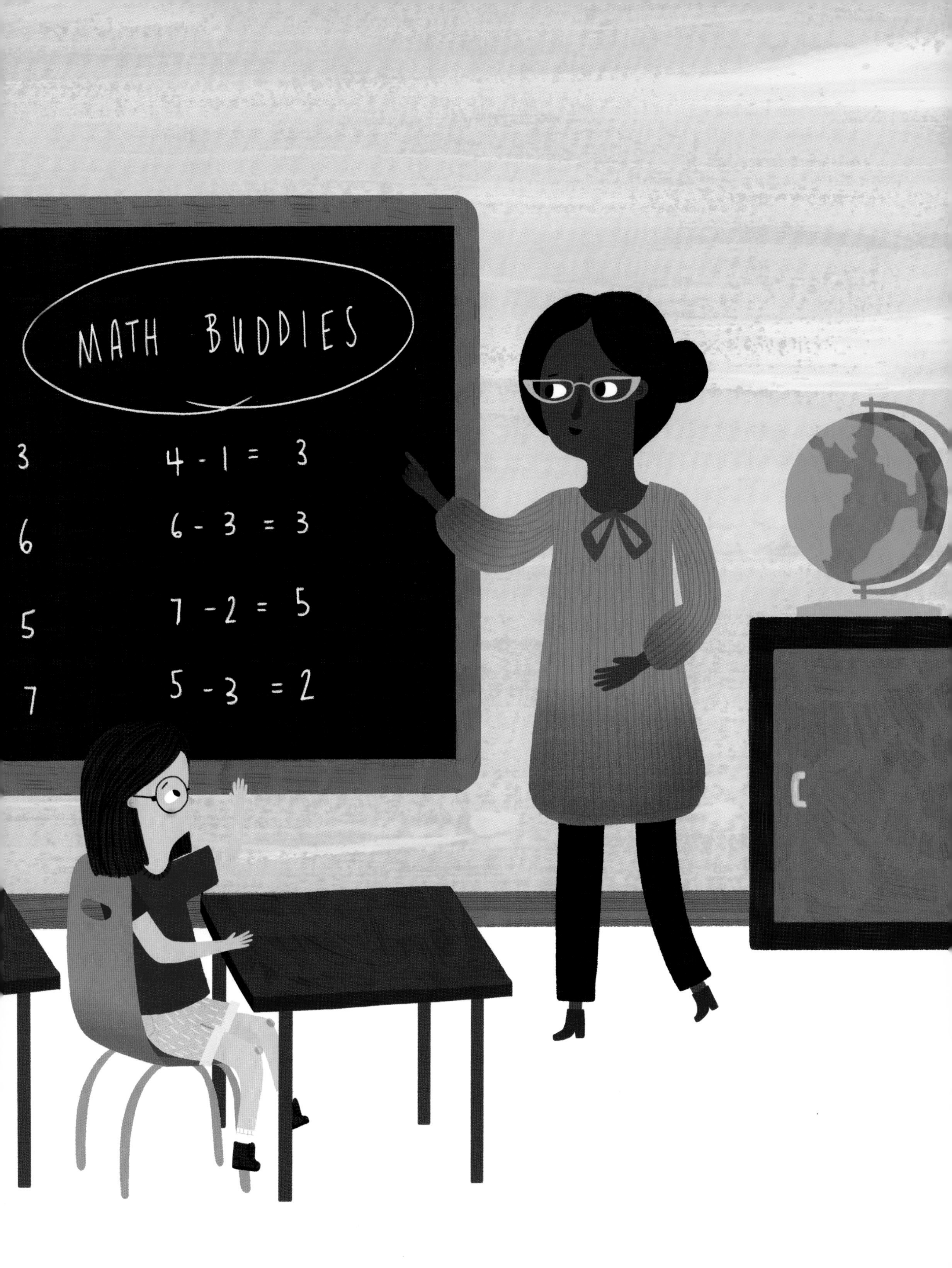
MATH BUDDIES
3
6
5
7
4 - 1 = 3
6 - 3 = 3
7 - 2 = 5
5 - 3 = 2

"You can do this," Adelaide whispered. "Come on."

Bear grunted and followed Adelaide.

"I know Bear was a wonderful reading buddy," said Mrs. Fitz-Pea. "But reading is one thing. Math? I'm not convinced."

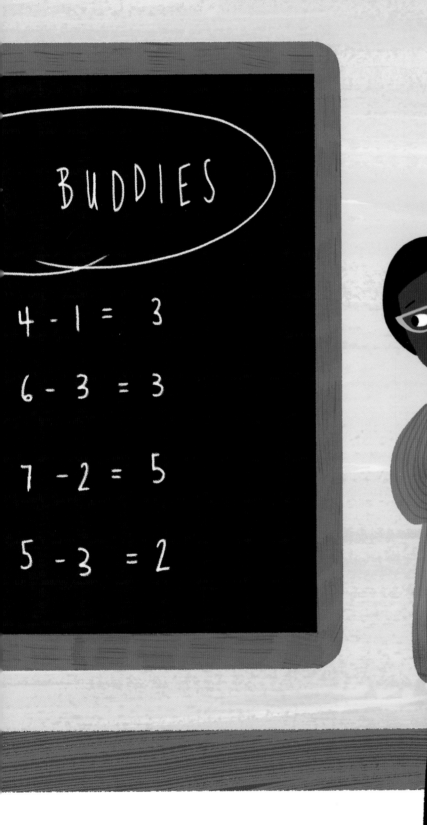

BUDDIES

$4 - 1 = 3$

$6 - 3 = 3$

$7 - 2 = 5$

$5 - 3 = 2$

"Bears make the best math buddies," said Adelaide. "It's simply a fact. They know how to put one paw in front of the other and measure any distance."

"Of course, they never get turned around. They know north is at 12 o'clock, east is at 3 o'clock, south is at 6 o'clock, and west is at 9 o'clock."

"Bears make the best math buddies because they have great imaginations. As the clouds drift by, they see every shape and every size from every angle. Circles, triangles, squares, and rectangles."

"Out on the river, catching fish takes practice. Bears never ever quit. Before long, the salmon add up."

$$1 + 1 + 1 + 2 = 5$$

"And sometimes they subtract."

$$5 - 2 = 3$$

"Bears make the best math buddies because every night they count the stars until they fall asleep."

1, 2, 3, 4, 5, 6, 7, 8, 9, 10 . . .

"In the morning, they're ravenous to collect lots of berries. But before they gobble them up . . .

. . . they sort them into groups so they can analyze their haul and sum up their rewards."

"Bears make the best math buddies because they know that not every answer comes easily. Sometimes you have to make a few mistakes, turn over a few rocks, and really dig deep to discover the solution."

"And when you get it right . . .

. . . they spring into action and

ROARRR!

Because they knew you
could do it all along."

"They know that whether you're in the classroom or out in the big wide world . . .

. . . math is everywhere. There's a pattern in everything. Solving puzzles is fun!"

"Is there anything this bear can't do?"
Mrs. Fitz-Pea asked.

$$1 + 2 = 3$$

$$1 + 3 = 4$$

$$1 + 4 = 5$$

$$2 + 2 = 4$$

2

"No," said Adelaide. "He understands the whole picture."

"Well, that sums up that problem," said Mrs. Fitz-Pea.

$$2 \times 2 = 4$$

$$2 \times 3 = 6$$

$$2 \times 4 = 8$$

$$2 \times 5 = 10$$

$$2 \times 6 = 12$$

"Do you think we should tell her that you're great at writing, too?" Adelaide asked.

Bear just grinned.

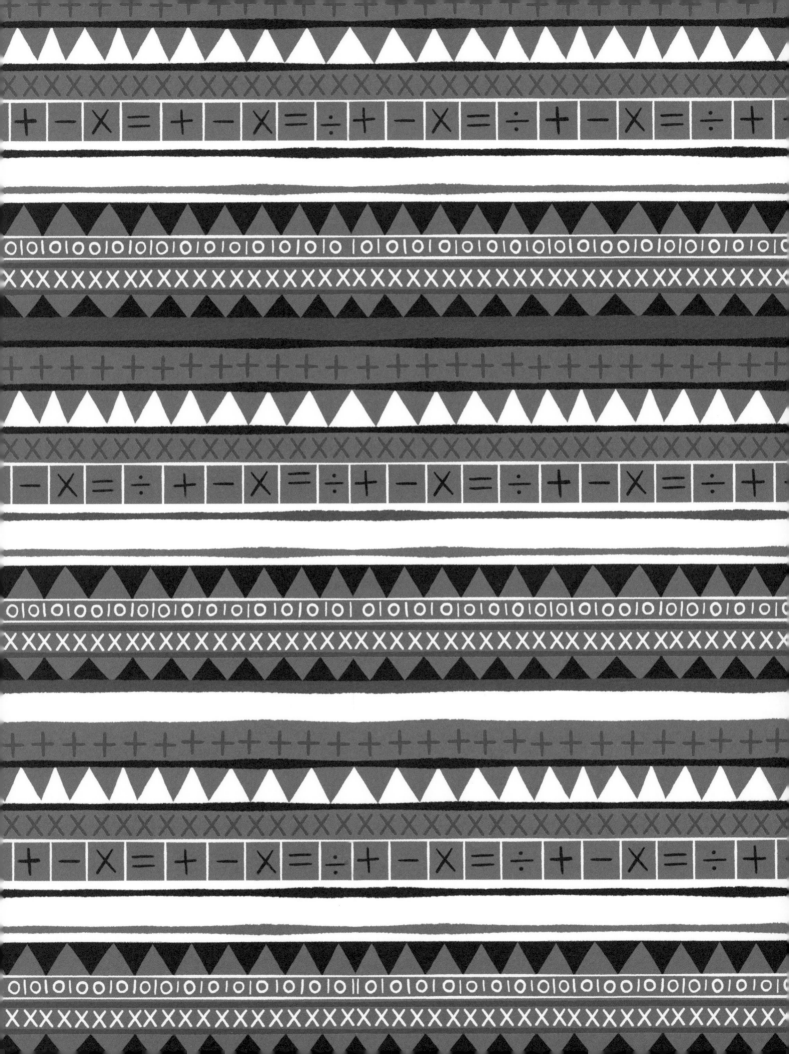

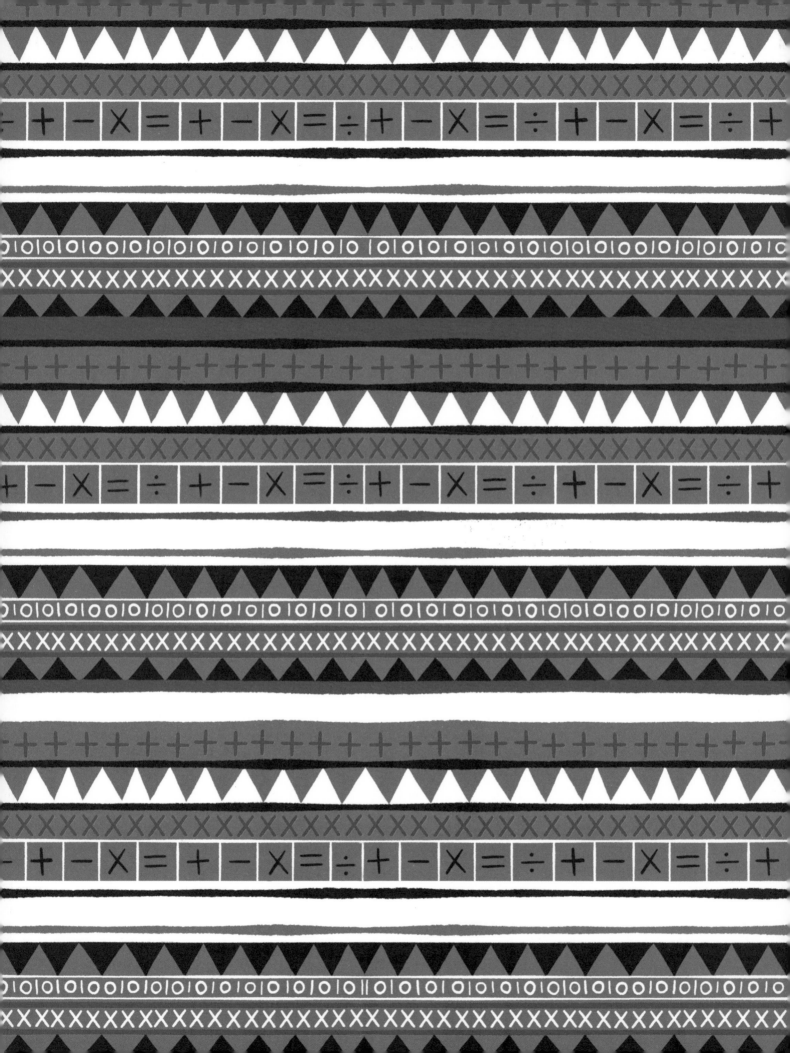